Table of Contents

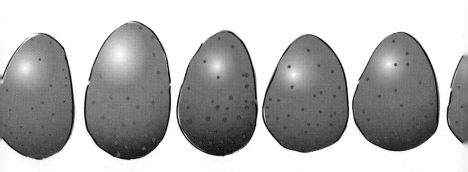

Meet Jane and Robert O'Connor

Jane and Robert O'Connor are a mother and son author team. Robert O'Connor came up with the idea for *Super Cluck* when he was only seven years old.

Meet Megan Lloyd

Megan Lloyd couldn't find the right henhouse to illustrate, so she built her own. Then she bought some chicks and hens and filled the henhouse with *Super Cluck* models. They became her pets!

Ms. Lloyd with a model, Chuck Cluck

SUPER CLUCK

by Jane O'Connor and Robert O'Connor
pictures by Megan Lloyd

HOUGHTON MIFFLIN COMPANY
BOSTON
ATLANTA DALLAS GENEVA, ILLINOIS PALO ALTO PRINCETON

Acknowledgments

Grateful acknowledgment is made for use of the following material:

Text

1 *Super Cluck,* by Jane O'Connor and Robert O'Connor, illustrated by Megan Lloyd. Text copyright © 1991 by Jane O'Connor and Robert O'Connor. Illustrations copyright © 1991 by Megan Lloyd. Reprinted by permission of HarperCollins Publishers. **65** "The Most Wonderful Egg in the World," a play adaptation of *The Most Wonderful Egg in the World,* by Helme Heine, from February 1994 *Super Science Red* magazine. Copyright © 1994 by Scholastic, Inc. Original English translation copyright © 1983 J.M. Dent and Sons, Ltd., London. Reprinted by permission of Scholastic, Inc. and Atheneum Publishers, a division of Simon & Schuster, Inc. **70** "Who?" from *Feathered Ones and Furry,* by Aileen Fisher, illustrated by Eric Carle. Text copyright © 1971 by Aileen Fisher. Illustrations copyright © 1971 by Eric Carle. Reprinted by permission of Aileen Fisher and HarperCollins Publishers.

Illustrations

65–69 Darcia Labrosse. **70** Eric Carle.

Photography

ii Courtesy of Jane O'Connor (t); courtesy of Megan Lloyd (b). **65** Kimberly Butler (cover). **70** Tony Scarpetta.

To Trinity School, Class of 1997
—R.O'C.

To Teddy and Jim
—J.O'C.

For Sue, Sweetie, and Chubbs!
—M.L.

Chuck Cluck looks like other chicks.

He goes *peep peep* like other chicks.

But he is not like other chicks.

He comes from another planet—

the planet Nestron.

5

He came to Earth

on a rocket ship

when he was just an egg.

6

"This is not the planet for us,"

the chicken leader said.

All the chickens got back

into the rocket ship.

All except one egg.

BUMP! BUMP! BUMP!

Soon a nice Earth chicken came along.

"This poor egg must be lost,"

she said.

She petted the egg's shell.

"There, there, dear," she said.

"I will take you to my coop.

I will sit on you until you hatch."

And that is just what she did.

"What a fine chick you have,

Mrs. Cluck,"

said another chicken.

"Yes," said Mrs. Cluck.

She gave her new chick a soft peck.

"I will call you Chuck."

Soon Mrs. Cluck saw that Chuck Cluck was not like the other chicks.

Chuck Cluck was always hungry.

"Ma, can I have another worm?"
Chuck asked.

"Dear, you have already eaten
537 worms this morning,"
Mrs. Cluck told him.

"But I am a growing chick,"
said Chuck.

"Yes, dear. That is true,"
said Mrs. Cluck.

"You keep growing and growing
and growing."

Chuck Cluck was very strong.

One day a corncob rolled

under the chicken coop.

Chuck picked up the chicken coop

to get it.

"Help! Help!

An earthquake!"

the chickens shouted.

15

Chuck put the coop down

and ran inside.

"There is no earthquake,"

he told the chickens.

"It was only me.

I did not mean to scare you."

"You must learn to be more careful,"

said Mrs. Cluck.

Chuck Cluck tried.

But it was not easy.

Once he pecked a hole so deep

five chicks fell into it.

Another time he sneezed so hard,

he blew feathers off the chickens.

"I cannot do anything right,"

Chuck said sadly.

But he was wrong!

19

One day all the chicks

were playing in the yard.

Three chicks jumped on Chuck.

"We got you!" they shouted.

"Ooh! Stop! Stop!" Chuck cried,

and he flapped his wings—hard.

21

"Look!" shouted the chicks.

"Chuck Cluck is flying!"

"What?" cried Chuck.

Then he looked down.

The ground was far away.

"Wow!" he shouted.

"I *am* flying!"

Chuck Cluck flapped his wings harder.

Up and up he went.

"Ma! Ma! I can fly!"

Chuck Cluck shouted.

Mrs. Cluck was so proud.

"Be careful, dear,"

she called up to him.

"Chuck Cluck is as fast

as a rocket,"

shouted one chick.

25

Chuck came in for a landing.

"Here he comes,"

cried another chick.

"It's Super Cluck!"

Chuck liked that name.

"Watch what Super Cluck will do now!"

he said.

"Look at this flip,"

Chuck shouted.

"Now I will do a tailspin.

And for my last trick,

I will do a loop-the-loop."

29

CRASH!

Chuck Cluck landed

in the vegetable patch.

All the other chicks laughed.

"You are a big show-off,"

said one chick.

"You are not Super Cluck.

You are a dumb cluck,"

said another chick.

"I am not!" yelled Chuck.

"I am Super Cluck.

Just wait.

I will show you."

31

The next morning

there was trouble

in the chicken coop.

"My egg is gone!"

cried one chicken.

"So is mine!" shouted another.

The chickens looked

in every nest.

Four eggs were missing.

The next day

three eggs were missing.

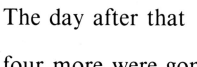

The day after that

four more were gone.

"Someone is stealing our eggs,"

said Mrs. Cluck.

"Aha!" thought Chuck.

"This is a job for Super Cluck."

35

That night Chuck stayed up late.

He waited and he watched.

Soon he saw a shadow

creep into the chicken coop.

36

The shadow had big ears,

a pointy nose,

and a long skinny tail.

Chuck Cluck had never seen

anything like it.

"Hee hee hee,"

the creature laughed softly.

"Let me see how many eggs

I can pop into my bag tonight."

"The egg thief!" said Chuck.

"I will follow him and see

where he takes these eggs.

The other eggs may be there too.

And I, Super Cluck,

will save them all!"

Chuck Cluck followed the creature

outside.

Chuck hid behind trees

and bushes and rocks.

He did not want the creature

to see him.

"Home at last!"

cried the creature.

"What a dump!"

Chuck said to himself.

Chuck hid behind an old red wagon

and watched.

43

The creature put the eggs

from his bag into a tire.

"…ten, eleven, twelve, thirteen,"

he counted. "Perfect!"

Then the creature

got out a frying pan

and made a big fire.

"Now for the cheese!"

he said.

The creature dragged out

a hunk of smelly cheese.

He started dancing

around his fire.

45

"The fire is hot,

and I have my cheese.

A little salt and pepper,

if you please.

Now in go the eggs—

all thirteen.

I'll cook the best omelet

the world has ever seen!"

48

Chuck ran out to the tire.

"Super Cluck will put a stop to this!"

he shouted to the eggs.

"Super who?" asked the creature.

Chuck Cluck scooped up the eggs

and got ready for takeoff.

"Watch out behind you!"

the creature shouted.

Chuck Cluck turned around.

THUNK!

The creature whacked him

with the frying pan.

"That is the oldest trick

in the book,

and you fell for it!"

the creature said with a laugh.

Chuck Cluck did not even feel it,

but all the eggs fell and cracked.

51

Chuck Cluck hid his face.

"Oh, no!" he cried.

"I broke all the eggs.

Some Super Cluck I am!"

"My omelet is ruined!"

shouted the creature.

Suddenly Chuck heard a noise.

Peep! Peep! Peep!

A little head popped out

of an egg.

Peep! Peep! Peep!

Out popped three more chicks.

Soon there were thirteen

little yellow balls of fuzz.

Chuck Cluck grabbed a basket.

"Hop in here!"

he told the little chicks.

"There is not a moment to lose."

The thirteen chicks

hopped inside the basket,

and Chuck Cluck took off.

The creature shook his fist.

"You got away this time,"

he shouted.

"But you have not seen

the last of me."

Soon Chuck Cluck

and the chicks were home.

Mrs. Cluck hugged Chuck.

He told her about

the creature.

"That was a rat,"

Mrs. Cluck told him,

"and I bet we have not seen

the last of him."

"That is just what he said, Ma,"

Chuck said.

"But for now

everyone is safe."

61

All the chicks cheered

and carried Chuck

around the chicken coop.

No one called Chuck

a dumb cluck anymore.

Now they shouted,

"Hooray for Super Cluck!"

The Most Wonderful Egg in the World

based on the book by Helme Heine

CHARACTERS
Narrator
The Three Hens: Dotty, Stalky, Plumy
King
Hen Chorus

NARRATOR: Once upon a time, three hens were
fighting. They were fighting about which of
them was the most beautiful.

DOTTY: I have the most beautiful feathers!

STALKY: I have the most beautiful legs!

PLUMY: I have the most beautiful crest on my head!

NARRATOR: They could not settle their fight.
So they asked the king for help.

KING: What you can do is more important than
what you look like! Whoever lays the most
wonderful egg, I will make a princess.

NARRATOR: First, Dotty sat down in the wet grass.

DOTTY: CACKLE! CACKLE!

NARRATOR: Dotty stood up. There lay an egg, snow-white, spotless, and perfectly shaped.

HEN CHORUS: It shimmers like marble!

KING: This is the most perfect egg I have ever seen!

HEN CHORUS: It is! It is!

NARRATOR: Then it was Stalky's turn.

HEN CHORUS: Poor Stalky. How can she lay a more perfect egg?

STALKY: CACKLE! CACKLE!

NARRATOR: Stalky got up. There lay an egg so big, an ostrich would have been jealous.

KING: This is the biggest egg I have ever seen!

HEN CHORUS: It is! It is!

NARRATOR: Then it was Plumy's turn.

HEN CHORUS: Poor, poor Plumy! How can she lay a more perfect or bigger egg?

PLUMY: CACKLE!

NARRATOR: Plumy got up. There lay a square egg with straight sides!

HEN CHORUS: Each side shines in a different color!

KING: This is the most fantastic egg I have ever seen!

HEN CHORUS: It is! It is!

NARRATOR: But which egg was the most wonderful? It was impossible to say.

KING: I have decided. Dotty, Stalky, and Plumy shall all be made princesses!

NARRATOR: From that day on, the three hens were the best of friends. And they went on laying the most wonderful eggs.

Who?

Who lives inside a house
that doesn't have a door?

It doesn't have a window
or light inside, what's more.

Who lives inside a house
with walls so frail and thin
that when he once comes out
he cannot go back in?

by Aileen Fisher